A CAITLYN DLOUHY BOOK 𝒜 atheneum ATHENEUM BOOKS FOR YOUNG READERS

New York London Toronto Sydney New Delhi

Cuddle Monkey

WORDS BY
Blake Liliane Hellman

PICTURES BY
Chad Otis

A ATHENEUM BOOKS FOR YOUNG READERS
atheneum

An imprint of Simon & Schuster Children's Publishing Division

1230 Avenue of the Americas, New York, New York 10020

Text copyright © 2020 by Blake Liliane Hellman

Illustrations copyright © 2020 by Chad Otis

All rights reserved, including the right of reproduction in whole or in part in any form.

ATHENEUM BOOKS FOR YOUNG READERS is a registered trademark of Simon & Schuster, Inc.

Atheneum logo is a trademark of Simon & Schuster, Inc.

For information about special discounts for bulk purchases, please contact

Simon & Schuster Special Sales at 1-866-506-1949 or business@simonandschuster.com.

The Simon & Schuster Speakers Bureau can bring authors to your live event.

For more information or to book an event, contact the Simon & Schuster Speakers Bureau

at 1-866-248-3049 or visit our website at www.simonspeakers.com.

Jacket design by Debra Sfetsios-Conover; interior design by Debra Sfetsios-Conover and Ann Bobco

The text for this book was set in Futuramano.

The illustrations for this book were rendered in pencil, ink, and digital paint.

Manufactured in China

1019 SCP

First Edition

10 9 8 7 6 5 4 3 2 1

Library of Congress Cataloging-in-Publication Data

Names: Hellman, Blake Liliane, author. | Otis, Chad, illustrator.

Title: Cuddle Monkey / Blake Liliane Hellman ; illustrated by Chad Otis.

Description: First edition. | New York : Atheneum, [2020] | "A Caitlyn Dlouhy Book." | Summary:

Lewis loves cuddling but his parents are busy with baby Owen, cuddling with toys does not work out,

and everyone at school is too busy for a cuddle.

Identifiers: LCCN 2018035520 | ISBN 9781534431171 (hardcover) | ISBN 9781534431188 (eBook)

Subjects: | CYAC: Hugging—Fiction. | Monkeys—Fiction. | Family life—Fiction. | Babies—Fiction.

Classification: LCC PZ7.1.H4468 Cud 2020 | DDC [E]—dc23

LC record available https://lccn.loc.gov/2018035520

TO STEVE
—B. L. H.

FOR MY TWO CUDDLE MONKEYS, CATHY AND CHARLIE
—C. O.

Lewis *LOVED* to cuddle!

After getting dressed he was ready for more cuddles.

But cuddle time was over.

This was *not* going to stop Cuddle Monkey.

He curled up
with his favorite book.

And some bananas.

And his favorite purple truck.

He even tried to cuddle a puddle
(just because it rhymed).

Not his best plan ever.

He waited for at least seventeen seconds.
Now it must be cuddle time, Lewis thought.

But *now* it was time for baby Owen's bath.

So, Lewis snuggled all his stuffed animals:

FLUFFY and ROCKY

and BIG CECILIA GRAY

and LITTLE CECILIA GRAY

and HEDWIG

and LAMBY

and KING KONG
THE GREAT

and MONSTER DUDE.

That didn't work out so well either.
None of them knew how to cuddle back.

This time, Lewis waited
six whole minutes.
Was it cuddle time now?

It was not. *Now* it was time to go to school.

His classmates were too busy
to cuddle.

His teacher told him to sit back down in his chair.

The lunch lady just gave him a snack.

And the janitor pointed to a sign:

Cuddling during work hours not allowed.

Lewis, however, was determined.

But cuddling the school bus driver was too dangerous.

And at dinner it was too messy.

After dinner Mama said,
"It looks like someone could use a hug."

"Lewis, I have a big
job for you," she said.

"You can teach Owen how to cuddle."

Not her best plan ever.

Owen was wiggly and squiggly
and definitely *not* a good cuddler.

So, Lewis tried a few bounces ...

and smooches ...

and even a cookie.

He had hope!

After he tucked Owen in, Lewis got into his jammies and jumped into bed.

"Is it cuddle time now?" he called.

"Yes, it is," said Papa, who gave him a great,
big good-night squeeze.

"It most definitely is!" said Mama, who gave Lewis an *even greater, bigger* good-night squeeze.

"I LOVE to cuddle!" said Lewis.
"We KNOW,"
said his mama and papa together.

Lewis couldn't wait to start again tomorrow.